One-Dog Sleigh

Mary Casanova ✳ pictures by Ard Hoyt

Farrar Straus Giroux ✳ New York

For Charlie, celebrating many fine
sleigh rides together —M.C.

To the Aydelotts,
with love —A.H.

Farrar Straus Giroux Books for Young Readers
175 Fifth Avenue, New York 10010

Text copyright © 2013 by Mary Casanova
Pictures copyright © 2013 by Ard Hoyt
Color separations by Bright Arts (H.K.) Ltd.
Printed in China by Macmillan Production (Asia) Ltd.,
Kowloon Bay, Hong Kong (supplier code 10)
Designed by Andrew Arnold
First edition, 2013
1   3   5   7   9   10   8   6   4   2

mackids.com

Library of Congress Cataloging-in-Publication Data
Casanova, Mary.
    One-dog sleigh / Mary Casanova ; pictures by Ard Hoyt. — 1st ed.
        p.   cm.
    Summary: A girl hitches her pony to her sleigh one morning, only to
be insistently joined by a series of animals, large and small.
    ISBN 978-0-374-35639-2 (hardcover)
    [1. Stories in rhyme.   2. Sleds—Fiction.   3. Animals—Fiction.
4. Snow—Fiction.]   I. Hoyt, Ard, ill.   II. Title.

PZ8.3.C267Ons 2013
[E]—dc23
                                                                2012007581

Farrar Straus Giroux Books for Young Readers may be purchased for
business or promotional use. For information on bulk purchases please
contact Macmillan Corporate and Premium Sales Department at
(800) 221-7945 x5442 or by email at specialmarkets@macmillan.com.

I hitched up my pony
to my little red sleigh.
My dog wagged his tail.
"I want to play!"

"You bet," I said. "Just me and you
in a one-dog sleigh."

My pony pranced off
under branches frosted white.
Squirrel chattered up above.
"I want to play!"

"We're well under way
in a one-dog sleigh."

But with a **LEAP**

and a **SPIN**,

Squirrel nestled in.

Harness bells sang
as we skimmed along the trail.
Owl **HOO-HOO-HOOTED**.
"I want to play!"

"Perhaps another day . . .
It's a one-squirrel, one-dog sleigh."

But on silent wings of gray,
Owl **SWOOPED** in to stay.

Runners of steel cut
through cedars dark and deep.
Lynx blinked from her sleep.
"I want to play!"

"Better not today . . .
It's a one-owl, one-squirrel, one-dog sleigh."

But with **MASSIVE** pads
and claws, Lynx landed on
soft paws.

We JING-JING-JINGLED along a winding ridge.
Deer lifted his head.
"I want to play!"

"Sorry, can't delay.
It's a one-lynx, one-owl, one-squirrel, one-dog sleigh."

But with a **CLATTER** of hoofed feet,
Deer crashed on our seat.

My pony pulled and pulled,
straining in her harness.
Bear snorted overhead.
"I want to play!"

"You'll stop us in our tracks.
It's a one-deer, one-lynx, one-owl,
one-squirrel, one-dog sleigh."

But with a **SMACK, CRACK, KA-WHACK!**
Bear balanced on the back.

Wind howled and scowled and blew mighty drifts of snow.
We jolted to a stop.

Mouse scampered up.
"I want to play!"

I started to cry.

"A blizzard's under way. And now we're stuck
in a one-mouse, one-bear, one-deer, one-lynx,
one-owl, one-squirrel, one-dog sleigh!"

Mouse stood tall on the dash.
"I'll lead the way!"

Then we all climbed out in the snow straightaway,
and we pushed and we tugged
on the little red sleigh.
Till we made it to the top . . .

in a one-pony, one-mouse, one-bear,
one-deer, one-lynx, one-owl,
one-squirrel, one-dog sleigh!

We flew the whole way . . .
till we hit a BUMP—

Then together we played
as the stars twinkled bright,
until we waved goodbye
on a crisp winter night.

We set off for home—
and a warm barn with hay—

just me and my pal
in a one-dog sleigh.